STICKS AND STONES
AND DOGGIE BONES

Read all the books about Barkley's School for Dogs!

Coming Soon!

BARKLEY'S
School
For Dogs

STICKS AND STONES
AND DOGGIE BONES

By Marcia Thornton Jones and Debbie Dadey

Illustrated by Amy Wummer

SCHOLASTIC INC.
New York Toronto London Auckland Sydney
Mexico City New Delhi Hong Kong Buenos Aires

To these great Werner Elementary students: Kellie Anderson, Nate Anderson, Rylee Billings, Brian Blackburn, Mikayla Bladow, Gregory Carron, Britlyn Compton, Becky Dadey, Carly Davis, Alex Johnson, Lea Johnson, Amanda Maciel, Lauren McGuinty, Drew Oswald, Eric Porter, Ryan Puccetti, Lanny Reed, Austin Roberts, Zac Roley, Alyssa Scimeca, Will Sherman, Jocelyn Thompson, Patrick Winters, and Jake Woodward. Special thanks to Jody Drager, a fun teacher!   —DD

To Helen Perelman and Emily Lo: two "howl-a-rrific" editors—and that's a Fido Fact.   —MTJ

ISBN 0-439-40838-5

12 11 10 9 8 7 6 5 4 3 2   2 3 4 5 6 7/0

Printed in the U.S.A.   40

First Scholastic printing, March 2002

Book design by Dawn Adelman

This book is set in 14-pt. Cheltenham.

Contents

THE GOOD LIFE

"Dog-awesome!" Bubba squealed and rolled on the ground. I had to admit, my little pup friend was right. For a dog, nothing felt better than to roll around in fresh green grass. I rolled and wiggled on the Barkley's School playground right along with Bubba. It was doggie heaven.

I'm Jack, a real Wonder Dog, and let me tell you that I'd much rather be home with my human, Maggie, protecting her from harm. But Maggie thought I needed to go to school to be a better, smarter dog. It

hurt my feelings more than a little. Still, on days like this, Barkley's wasn't so bad.

"You fellows sure look happy," my good friend Blondie said.

"It's howl-a-rrific!" Bubba said. "Try it."

I tried not to laugh. Blondie was a beautiful poodle. No, she was more than that. Blondie was the most beautiful poodle in the world, and she was definitely not the type to roll around on the grass.

I guess I didn't know Blondie as well as I thought. She plopped down on the grass and wiggled beside Bubba. "Don't mind if I do," Blondie said. She had the biggest poodle grin on her face that I'd ever seen.

Before long, the whole play yard had dogs rolling around on the grass in the bright sunshine. It was a happy sight.

Yes, everything was hunky-dory at Barkley's School for Dogs, but it didn't last. "Move out of my way," Sweetcakes growled at Bubba. Poor Bubba hopped

up and ran to the other side of the yard.
Sweetcakes is one big bully.

Her sidekick, Clyde, the bulldog,
echoed, "Yeah, move it."

I wanted to tell Sweetcakes she didn't
own this yard. I wanted to tell Sweetcakes
that Bubba was there first, but I didn't.
Sweetcakes is not exactly the kind of
Doberman pinscher who listens to rea-
son. She's the kind of dog who would bite

off your ear instead. In fact, Sweetcakes had lost part of her own ear in a fight. I really didn't want to lose any of my body parts today.

I hung my head and said nothing. It pained my brain, let me tell you. Not standing up for Bubba did not fit my Wonder Dog image.

Bubba huddled beside an older dog named Woodrow. They both looked at me to see what I would do. I was about to

open my mouth to growl at Sweetcakes when Floyd arrived. Floyd was a great beagle buddy of mine, and he's the nicest dog you'd ever want to meet.

Today he looked a lot different. In fact, when Blondie saw him, she yelped, "Oh, my gosh! What happened to you?"

OPERATION

Usually, Floyd was a happy-go-lucky kind of dog, but not today. Floyd looked pitiful. In fact, I'd never seen him looking so sad.

"I had an operation on my nose," Floyd said in a funny voice, as if someone had pinched his snout shut.

"Oh, you poor thing," Blondie said. "Are you going to be all right?"

Floyd nodded. "The worst is over, but the doctor says I have to wear this collar for a few days."

A big white collar circled Floyd's neck.

It was plastic and looked like a huge ice cream cone. Bubba came up beside Floyd and giggled. "Floyd," Bubba asked, "are you dressed up for Halloween?"

Pups ask a lot of questions, so I knew Bubba didn't mean anything by it. Still, it seemed that Floyd's ears drooped a little more than usual. Blondie noticed it, too.

"Shh," Blondie said softly to Bubba. "You'll hurt Floyd's feelings."

"It's all right," Floyd told Bubba. "I have to wear this to keep from scratching the stitches out."

"It looks uncomfortable," I said.

Floyd nodded, and the white collar swayed up and down. "It's really hard to take a nap. I feel like I'm stuck in a bowl."

"You look like a foghorn," Sweetcakes growled.

Clyde chuckled from beside Sweet-cakes, "Yeah, yeah. Foghorn."

Floyd hung his head, and I hoped

Sweetcakes would leave Floyd alone. We weren't so lucky. Sweetcakes tapped Floyd's plastic collar with her paw.

"This thing makes you look even sillier than usual. In fact, this looks like a clown collar from the circus. That's it, Floyd the Clown."

"Yeah. Clown," Clyde panted.

I opened my mouth to tell Sweetcakes to leave Floyd alone, but Sweetcakes snarled at me, and I backed up. Chills went up and down my backbone.

Sweetcakes looked as if she could eat me alive, and she probably could have. I gulped and said nothing.

Thankfully, Sweetcakes decided it was time to get a drink, and she left. I sank to the ground and put my paws over my eyes. I had failed both Floyd and Bubba today. What was wrong with me? Why hadn't I stood up for them? Had I lost my Wonder Dog power?

I lifted one paw to look at Floyd. Usually Floyd chewed on a toy or ball, but today he sat staring into space. His brown eyes puddled with tears.

"Don't pay attention to Sweetcakes and Clyde," Blondie told Floyd. "Those were only words. Words can't really hurt you."

That reminded me of something I had heard Maggie, my human, say. "Blondie is right," I yipped. "Remember, sticks and stones may break your bones, but words can never hurt you."

"Sticks?" Bubba interrupted. "Stones? Doggie bones? Where? Where? I'd like to chase them! And chew on some juicy bones!"

Blondie nudged Bubba with her black nose. "There aren't any sticks and stones and doggie bones. But I believe I see a ball over there."

Bubba didn't need to have it pointed out twice. He galloped after the ball. "Come on," Bubba called to Floyd. "Let's play."

Floyd shook his head and looked at the ground, but Bubba wouldn't take no for an answer. The pup threw the ball at Floyd. Unfortunately, the ball landed right inside Floyd's plastic collar. It rolled down and lodged next to his floppy ear.

"Help!" Floyd whimpered. "It's stuck!"

I raced over and pulled out the ball.

"Thanks," Floyd mumbled.

"No problem," I said. "It could happen to anyone."

Floyd nodded, and the collar bobbed up and down.

"Do you want to get some water with me?" I asked Floyd, trying to get his mind off the collar.

Floyd shook his head, sighed, and wandered off toward the back of the yard where there were lots of trees. Every dog needs time alone. I figured this was one of those times for Floyd.

I wasn't so sure Maggie, my human, was right. Mean words couldn't break bones like sticks and stones, but words could hurt. It was a Fido Fact—I could tell by looking at Floyd as he plodded across the play yard.

I took my eyes off him for only one second. One second was all it took. I could not believe what happened.

SOMETHING ELSE

"AAA-RROOOOO! AAA-RROOOOO!" Floyd's howl rattled the windows of Barkley's School for Dogs.

Ears twitched and hair bristled when Floyd howled again.

Floyd needed help, and I, Jack, the Wonder Dog, could not let him down. I bolted across the yard. When Floyd howled a third time, every one of Floyd's pals joined me. Unfortunately, so did Sweetcakes, Clyde, and about seventeen other dogs.

I jumped over Casanova the Chihuahua
and squeezed between two Irish setters,
Rhett and Scarlett, to come nose-to-nose
with Floyd. Blondie was right behind me.

"Oh, dear," Blondie said with a whine.

"What happened?" Bubba asked as he
squeezed under my belly to get a good
look. "What is Floyd doing between those
trees? Why is he howling?"

"Let's stay calm," Blondie interrupted,

"and let's not ask any more questions." I tried to be calm and looked at Floyd.

It was a Fido Fact that these trees at Barkley's School for Dogs were dog-awesome because they were so close together. They made a perfect hideaway for a sad dog. Unfortunately, one sad dog had forgotten about one thing—his collar.

"Now that's what I call one stuck pup," Sweetcakes said as she pushed her way to the front of the crowd.

"Yeah," Clyde mumbled. "Stuck pup."

For once, I had to admit Sweetcakes was right. Floyd's collar was wedged between two trees, tighter than a cork in a bottle.

"Get me out of here," Floyd whimpered.

I had already failed my friends two times. I had to redeem myself. "Wonder Dog to the rescue," I barked. I tried to make myself sound full of confidence.

Sweetcakes didn't buy it. Neither did

Floyd, which hurt more than just a little.

"Looks like Floyd's going to be there a long, long time," Sweetcakes said with a slobbery laugh.

"Maybe you should get Fred," Floyd whimpered. Fred Barkley was the human in charge of Barkley's School for Dogs.

Floyd lifted his nose and howled. *"AAA-RRRRRRRRROOOOOO!"*

It was time to do my Wonder Dog work. I grabbed Floyd's plastic collar and tugged. The collar slipped out of my mouth. I tried three more times. No luck. The collar was just too slick to sink my teeth into.

I tilted my head, first one way, then the other to get a better look at the situation. My friend Floyd was counting on me, Jack the Wonder Dog. I had to try one more time. That's when Sweetcakes took a giant step toward me. It was doggie instinct that made me jump back.

"We'll be here all day if we wait for you," Sweetcakes snarled. And then she did the impossible. Sweetcakes gripped Floyd's plastic collar in a death grip and pulled. Hard. Floyd popped loose and tumbled to the ground.

"Th-th-thanks," Floyd stammered.

Sweetcakes snarled, showing one long yellow fang. "I didn't do it for you, Clown-Face," she told Floyd. "I did it for me. Your howling was disturbing my beauty rest. Now, get out of my sight."

The dogs in Barkley's play yard scattered faster than a wag of a tail.

"I can't believe Sweetcakes helped Floyd," Blondie said.

Floyd watched Sweetcakes circle a napping spot. "Maybe, just maybe, Sweetcakes isn't so bad after all," Floyd said.

His words hurt me all the way down to my toenails. It was bad enough that Sweetcakes was Floyd's new hero, but something else was even worse.

I had let my friends down for the third time in one day.

MONSTER MOVIE

I needed something to chew on. Sinking my teeth into nice soft leather is the perfect way to think over a problem. I was sniffing around for an old shoe when the door to Barkley's School swung open.

Fred Barkley rang a bell that could mean only one thing. Lessons. Juicy reward treats were just the thing to make a sad pup forget his troubles. Twenty dogs darted across the yard. Even Floyd trotted over to Fred.

I raced to the front, stopping long

enough to tell Harry the Westie I was sorry for knocking him over. I stood between Blondie and my pal Woodrow. Then I made my brown eyes as sad as I could. This always works with Maggie, and she gives me an extra treat. Unfortunately, Fred didn't seem to notice.

Fred did not believe in giving dogs something for nothing. He expected us to work for our treats. Scattered throughout the play yard was equipment made just for dogs. There were tunnels to run through, a teeter-totter to balance on, and bars to jump over. Sweetcakes was a pro at all of it, and she had a wall full of ribbons to prove it. The rest of us needed practice, and that's just what Fred had us do.

I must admit, I couldn't figure out why Fred wanted me to run through tunnels when they were so much fun to jump over. He kept trying to get me to dart inside them, and I kept showing him how much faster it was to jump over them. Finally he scratched my ears and told me to have a seat.

Floyd was ready to do whatever Fred wanted. He held his head high so his collar wouldn't trip him as he headed for the opening in the tunnel. "Not today, Floyd," Fred said, reaching out and scratching Floyd's drooping ears. "You have to be extra careful with your collar. You get to sit this one out."

"What a useless dog," Sweetcakes muttered as she pranced past.

"Yeah," Clyde said. "Useless.

We were panting by the time Fred finally decided we'd had enough practice. Everyone, that is, except Floyd. He had stayed where Fred told him to sit and watched us. He had trouble turning his head because the collar kept getting in his way.

Finally, Fred called us to our treat bowls. There were so many wagging tails, you had to watch to make sure your nose didn't get smacked. Sweetcakes's treats were gone in the blink of an eye, and mine didn't last much longer. That's when I noticed Floyd was having trouble getting to his treats. The collar kept scooting them out of his reach.

"I'll help you with that," Sweetcakes told Floyd.

We all stared as Sweetcakes trotted

over to Floyd. Nobody twitched a muscle when Sweetcakes smiled. Then, without batting an eyelash, Sweetcakes bent down and gobbled up every last bit of Floyd's treats.

"Hey!" Floyd whined. "Those were my treats."

"That wasn't very nice at all," Blondie blurted.

"Why did Sweetcakes do that?" Bubba asked.

"Because," I said with a snarl, "Sweetcakes is mean."

Sweetcakes looked at the rest of the dogs and smiled, but it wasn't a friendly smile at all. "Any more dogs need help with their snacks?" she asked.

Every last one of us backed up. Every one, that is, except Woodrow.

Woodrow was not what you would call a young basset hound. He wasn't the fastest dog in the yard either, but he made up for it by being the bravest. Woodrow walked right up to Sweetcakes. "We don't need your kind of help," he told her.

And then Woodrow proved he was just as nice as he was brave. He gave Floyd the rest of his treats.

"Thanks, Woodrow," Floyd said.

"My pleasure," Woodrow said before heading for the pile of rags by the door for his nap.

"I'm going to be nice, too," Bubba said as he took the rest of his treats to Floyd. "Just like Woodrow."

"That," I told Bubba, "is an excellent idea."

I looked down at my empty bowl. I had nothing left to give Floyd. I had let my friend down once more.

Floyd was eating one of Bubba's snacks when Sweetcakes and Clyde started giggling.

"Look at Funnel Face," Sweetcakes said. "That sore on his nose is the prettiest thing about him."

"Yeah," Clyde repeated. "Funnel Face."

"With a face like that," Sweetcakes said loud enough to reach every floppy ear, "Floyd could be in the movies—a monster movie."

"Monster movie," Clyde said with a snicker.

Enough was enough. Sweetcakes had caused trouble for everyone.

I jumped in front of Sweetcakes. She had to be stopped, and I was the dog to stop her!

UNDERWEAR DOG

I must have lost my mind for a minute, because I growled. I growled at Sweet-cakes. It wasn't a little growl under my breath. No, I did a full-face, open-jawed, hair-raised-up-on-my-back growl.

I think I scared Bubba. He ran and hid behind a tree, but Sweetcakes laughed. I mean really laughed. "Are you growling at me, Underwear Dog?" Sweetcakes sneered.

Clyde snickered. "Yeah, Underwear Dog."

"That's *Wonder* Dog," I barked to

Sweetcakes. "And yes, I'm growling at you. I've had enough of your picking on my friend."

Sweetcakes stuck her nose right next to mine. I could smell Floyd's stolen treats on her breath, and it made me madder. "Listen, Underwear Dog," Sweetcakes growled. "I'll do what I want when I want. You got it?"

"Yeah. Yeah," Clyde panted.

Sweetcakes knocked her nose against mine. Let me tell you it hurt, but I wasn't about to show it. It was showdown time. It was high noon at Barkley's School for Dogs, and I was challenging Sweetcakes to a fight. It wasn't something I wanted to do, but I had to for my friends.

Luckily, Blondie was watching out for me. "Sweetcakes," Blondie called out. "Fred wants you at the back door."

Sweetcakes bared her teeth at me. "I won't forget about this. I'll get you."

Clyde barked over his shoulder as he followed Sweetcakes. "Yeah, yeah."

My perfect morning had turned to mush. I sat down by the brick wall. Floyd, Bubba, and Blondie came and sat next to me. As bad as things were for me, they were worse for Floyd. He really looked uncomfortable.

"Sweetcakes is right," Floyd said. "This collar makes me look like a clown."

"All dogs look like clowns when they're

pushed around," a high-pitched voice interrupted. "That collar has nothing to do with it."

"Who said that?" Bubba yipped and turned in a complete circle. "Whose voice is that?"

SPY

"Calm down," I said. "It's only Tazz."

Bubba stopped running in circles and tilted his head to look up. There, sprawled on the top of the wall, was the hairiest black-and-gold cat in the entire city. Her tail swept lazily back and forth, just out of reach.

The dogs at Barkley's knew about Tazz. She lived in the neighborhood and had a habit of causing trouble for us canine friends.

"How long have you been spying on us?" Blondie asked.

"Long enough to watch Underwear Dog here get his nose bruised," Tazz purred.

"That's *Wonder* Dog!" I howled. I took several deep breaths. Tazz had a way of getting on a dog's last nerve.

"Jack doesn't have a problem with his nose," Bubba yipped, "but Floyd does."

Floyd sighed. He tried to lie down, but his collar hit the ground. "This collar makes me useless," he said, "and ugly. Just as Sweetcakes said."

"You look like a typical dog, if you ask me. Let me show you what real beauty is," Tazz said. She stood up and walked along the top of the wall, swishing her tail in the sunlight. "Look at this glorious tail. See how fluffy it is?"

Bubba looked back at his own tail. "My tail goes back and forth," he said.

Tazz squinted at Bubba's tail. It was wagging so fast it looked like a blur. "A dog's tail is no match for a cat's," Tazz said.

Tazz's words ruffled the hair on my neck. After all, my own tail is a wonderful sight, if I do say so myself. I was just about to tell Tazz that when Woodrow waddled up.

"What's the cat doing here?" Woodrow asked. That was just like Woodrow. He never let anything bother him. Not even a cat.

Tazz stopped pacing along the top of the wall. She crouched down and glared at Woodrow and then looked at Floyd. "I'm here to help you, which is more than your friends here are doing."

Floyd hopped up, front paws on the wall, and yelped. "My friends have helped," he told Tazz. "They're good friends. Woodrow even shared his treats with me."

Tazz looked down her nose at Floyd.

"So," she said. "You're trying to tell me that you don't mind being teased by Sweetcakes?"

Floyd lowered his head. "No one likes being called names," he said.

Woodrow stepped forward. "Words can only hurt you if you let them." He slowly moved back to his rag pile for more rest.

We all knew Woodrow was right, but I still couldn't stop thinking about Tazz's comment about being no help to Floyd. I didn't want to let down my friend anymore. I was now a dog with a plan!

DOGGIE DOUBTS

I wasn't so sure my plan would work. In fact, I had big doggie doubts. I wrinkled my forehead in a frown. "My plan will take teamwork," I told my friends after I told them about it.

Woodrow nodded and his ears swept across the grass.

"Not just between us, either," I added. "Every dog at Barkley's will need to bite into the plan if we want this to work."

Floyd still looked a little sad.

Blondie nudged Floyd with her nose.

44

"We can do it, I know we can. Right, Jack?"

Blondie turned her brown eyes on me. "Of course, the plan will work."

"That's the spirit," Woodrow said. "Let's get busy."

Getting all the dogs at Barkley's to agree to my plan was about as easy as herding kittens. Dogs eyed us as if we were trying to take them to the veterinarian.

"No way," Harry the Westie said.

"Are you out of your doggie brains?" Casanova the Chihuahua asked.

"You must be nuts. Totally bonkers," the two Irish setters, Rhett and Scarlett, decided.

"We won't know until we try," Blondie told them.

"You think this plan will work?" a little dog with a bald patch on his rump asked me.

I must admit. I wasn't sure my brilliant plan was that brilliant. In fact, the more we tried to convince the other dogs, the more I started thinking that the plan was about as easy as getting fleas to walk on a leash.

Blondie, Woodrow, and Floyd looked at me, along with the other dogs, waiting for my answer. "It won't hurt to try," I finally said. "Being a true friend means giving a one-hundred-percent try."

Fred Barkley interrupted our doggie talk. "Heel!" he yelled.

Fred is pretty good for a human, but he has this thing about his feet. Of course, Sweetcakes rushed to Fred and sat down by his feet. Clyde wasn't far behind.

Blondie blocked the rest of the dogs from following them. "Are you with us?" she asked.

Harry scratched at a flea. Casanova tried to dart between Bubba's legs. Rhett

and Scarlett whispered to each other.

It seemed that most of the dogs in the yard were avoiding our plan like medicine. It was going to take a Wonder Dog to convince them. "If I prove it can work, will you help us?" I asked.

The rest of the pooches thought a full seven seconds. Finally, Casanova stepped up. "Prove that your idea works," he said, "and we're in."

THE PLAN

Just thinking about what we were about to do made my tongue hang out. "I hope this will work, Woodrow," I mumbled as we made our way to Fred.

Woodrow loped along beside me. "Don't worry," he said. "I'm right beside you."

I looked down at Woodrow. He was slow and old, but it did help to know he was on my side. Woodrow was that kind of dog. He made you feel good just by being there.

Fred made us line up. Lining up twenty

dogs can take a while. Usually I tried to be at the front of the line, hoping I'd be first to get a treat. Today, however, I stepped aside.

"After you, Sweetcakes," I said in my most polite voice.

Sweetcakes looked down her pointy nose at me. "Of course I'm going first," she snarled. "I *always* go first."

She was right about that. Sweetcakes usually trampled any dog in her way, but today we all stepped aside.

Fred pointed to a balance beam. Let's

get this straight. Dogs don't like high places, but Fred didn't seem to understand that.

The balance beam was as tall as Fred. There were ramps at each end of the beam: one ramp to go up and the other ramp to come down. The foot of each ramp was painted yellow. Every dog knew that you were supposed to touch the yellow part, but we were usually too worried about being up so high to remember.

"Watch a pro at work," Sweetcakes bragged. Always ready to show off, she ran to the ramp, being sure to touch the yellow part near the grass.

I was tempted to snarl, but Woodrow nudged my side, reminding me of the plan—sweeten up Sweetcakes with kindness.

"Go, Sweetcakes," I mumbled.

"Louder," Blondie said. "Or she won't hear us."

"Go, Sweetcakes," I tried again. But cheering for Sweetcakes was not something I really wanted to do, so it came out like a whimper.

"I'll help," Bubba offered.

Sweetcakes was halfway across the balance beam when Bubba let out a howl that would stop a bus. "GO, SWEET-CAKES!"

I had to admit, the little pup had the heart of a lion. I also had to admit that my plan might work, because as soon as Sweetcakes heard Bubba, she froze.

"GO, SWEETCAKES!" Bubba cheered again in dog talk, and this time I joined him.

"Huh?" Sweetcakes muttered.

"What's the matter?" Fred asked her before we had a chance to howl out another cheer. "Are you afraid of being so high?"

"Afraid?" Sweetcakes repeated from

her place at the top of the balance beam.

Sweetcakes glared down at all of us. "I am *not* scared," she snarled. She glanced our way one more time before hurrying to the other end of the balance beam.

"Yay, Sweetcakes," Blondie, Woodrow, Bubba, and I all cheered as Sweetcakes started down the ramp. We tried to cheer as loud as we could.

Sweetcakes was so surprised she forgot to touch the yellow part of the ramp. Every dog knew that if you didn't touch that yellow part, Fred would make you go across the balance beam again. Sweetcakes had never had to do the balance beam twice—until today.

"Try again," Fred told Sweetcakes as he gently led her back to the on-ramp. Sweetcakes looked as if she were being dragged to a bath.

"Huh?" Sweetcakes yelped.

Sweetcakes was more confused than

ever. We cheered just as hard for her the second time. A few more dogs joined in. By the time Sweetcakes got across the balance beam, we were cheering so loud she was shaking.

"What's going on?" she demanded after we'd all given the balance beam our best shot, and Fred had dished out three treats apiece.

Blondie batted her eyelashes. "Nothing,

Sweetcakes. We were just rooting for the champion dog at Barkley's."

Woodrow nodded. "We wanted you to know we think you're the best dog at balancing on that beam."

"Here," Bubba said as he shoved his treats toward Sweetcakes. "Have my treats."

Sweetcakes took a giant step away from Bubba.

"You can have mine, too," Floyd said. "They're too hard for me to eat anyway, what with my big ugly nose and all."

I don't mind saying, what I did next wasn't easy. I looked at my three tasty morsels. Treats. They're what a dog lives for—that rich, meaty flavor bursting on our tongues. I sighed. My tail drooped so low it dragged on the ground. Then I looked up at Sweetcakes and smiled. Yes, I smiled at Sweetcakes.

"Take my treats, too," I said through my teeth. Then, very slowly, I pushed my treats straight toward Sweetcakes.

TRiCK TREATS

"What's wrong with the treats?" Sweetcakes snapped. "Are they poison?"

"Would we offer you treats with poison?" Blondie asked. She looked completely innocent when she batted her long eyelashes.

"Yes," Sweetcakes snapped. She had a point, but today we were trying to soften Sweetcakes with kindness. Being nice just wasn't working.

"Did you slobber all over them?" Sweetcakes growled.

I admit I got a little mad. After all, I wanted to eat my treats. "These treats are perfectly fine," I snapped. "Watch." I grabbed one of the treats and gulped it down. It was delicious.

"That's probably a trick treat," Sweetcakes growled. "The rest are rotten."

A trick treat! I had never heard of such a thing, although it sounded like a good thing for Halloween. I felt like telling Sweetcakes exactly how I felt about her and her silly trick treats.

Luckily, Woodrow thought of something nice to say. "We wanted to give you a present," Woodrow explained, "to show you how much we like you."

Sweetcakes growled. "You don't like me and you never have. All of you dogs are up to something, but I'm too smart for you. You'll never get me!" With that, Sweetcakes glared at Woodrow before darting up the teeter-totter.

Bubba shook his little puppy head. "Sweetcakes is so used to other dogs not liking her, she can't believe we're just trying to be nice."

It was sad, but true. Sweetcakes balanced in the middle of the teeter-totter, staring at all of us.

It made her nervous. A nervous dog on a teeter-totter is not a good thing. Sweetcakes was usually an expert on the

teeter-totter, but not today. One giant paw slipped off the edge, and the teeter-totter wiggled. That's when the unthinkable happened.

Blondie closed her eyes, and I let out a gasp. Sweetcakes slid off the teeter-totter and crashed to the ground.

NORMAL

"Quick!" Blondie barked. "Get help!

She didn't have to ask me, Jack, the Wonder Dog, twice. I rushed to the back door and scratched. Nothing. I looked over at Sweetcakes. She hadn't moved.

I had a terrible feeling in my tummy, and it wasn't from missing my treats. I was truly worried about Sweetcakes. This was important. I barked for Fred. Where was he? Couldn't he hear that we needed him?

"Let me help," Floyd barked. It didn't

matter that Floyd's nose was bandaged or that he was wearing a collar. It didn't matter that Sweetcakes had made fun of him. Floyd was ready to help.

Together, Floyd and I howled. Floyd's howl was magnificent, but still Fred didn't open the door.

"Everyone together!" Woodrow snapped. All the dogs in the yard lifted their snouts and howled in unison. Frankly, it was so

beautiful it brought tears to my eyes.

Fred finally opened the back door. "What's going on here?" he asked. All the dogs backed up to show Sweetcakes lying on the ground. Fred rushed over to Sweetcakes and gently examined her.

I breathed a sigh of relief when Sweetcakes licked Fred's hand. "She's all right," I barked, and all the other dogs let out a howl of relief.

Later that day, Bubba and I rolled in the grass. Life was sweet once more at Barkley's School for Dogs. At least, it was for everyone but Sweetcakes.

Sweetcakes had scratched her nose when she fell off the teeter-totter. It wasn't a terrible scratch. It must've really stung at first, but Sweetcakes gritted her teeth and refused to whimper when Fred cleaned it off and bandaged it. Too bad Sweetcakes didn't stop herself from scratching at it. Fred knew what Sweetcakes needed—a plastic collar, just like Floyd's.

I wanted to tell Sweetcakes that she looked like a circus clown. But then I remembered how Floyd had looked when Sweetcakes had said that to him.

Sticks and stones and bad words all did hurt—just in different ways. I didn't say a word . . . and neither did Sweetcakes.

Floyd came up beside me. "Thanks for

being such a great friend, Jack," he said. "You really came through for me."

My tail wagged back and forth. Having good friends was even better than rolling around in the grass in the warm after-noon sun.

ABOUT THE AUTHORS

Marcia Thornton Jones and Debbie Dadey used to work together at the same elementary school—Marcia taught in the classroom and Debbie was a librarian. But now they love writing about a totally different kind of school . . . where the students have four legs and a tail!

Marcia lives in Lexington, Kentucky, and Debbie lives in Fort Collins, Colorado. Their own pets have inspired them to write about Jack and his friends at Barkley's School. These authors have also written The Adventures of the Bailey School Kids, The Bailey City Monsters, and the Triplet Trouble series together.